# THIS BOOK
# BELONGS TO

_____

# The Adventures of
# Bella & Harry
## Let's Visit Vancouver!

Written by
## Lisa Manzione

Illustrated by
## Kristine Lucco

Bella & Harry, LLC

Swish!... Swish!

"Faster, Bella, faster!"

"**Whew!** That was a great snowboard run.
I just love snowboarding on Grouse Mountain."

"Harry, did you know Grouse Mountain is only about fifteen minutes from the City of Vancouver in British Columbia, Canada? The mountain is one of the North Shore Mountains of the Pacific Ranges in Canada."

**"Nope.** I did not know that. All I know is I LOVE snowboarding on Grouse Mountain. Bet I can beat you down the mountain."

**Swish.** Swishhhhhhhh.

"I win, Bella!"

8

"**Let's** go, Harry. We are leaving
Grouse Mountain now and heading back to
the City of Vancouver. Along the way, we will
stop at the Capilano Suspension Bridge Park."

"Sounds like fun!  Hmm...Bella, what is
a 'suspension bridge'?"

9

"**A** suspension bridge is a bridge that usually hangs from ropes or cables, and is attached to the ground at the beginning and end of the bridge."

"Let's run across the bridge."

"**The** bridge stretches about 450 feet across (about 75 moose standing tail-to-tail) and is about 230 feet above the Capilano River. The bridge was originally built in 1889. The park has other fun sights too."

11

"**Harry,** this park is one of the best sights near Vancouver. We can visit the Treetops Adventure while we are here. The Treetops Adventure will take us up 100 feet into the rainforest on suspension bridges attached to Douglas fir trees that are more than 250 years old. We can learn all about the temperate rainforest (woodlands that have a mild climate and heavy rainfall) and the ecosystem."

"How cool!"

12

"**Bella,** what is an 'ecosystem'?"

"An ecosystem is a place where living things interact with things around it."

13

"Whoa! What are these?"

"**Harry,** those are totem poles."

"'Totem poles'? What are totem poles, Bella?"

15

"**Authentic** totem poles are carved by hand out of one piece of wood. Totem poles are painted with pictures (symbols, figures, or masks) that relate to different Native American tribes or groups of people. The poles tell stories. Look at this pole, Harry. This is the 'Raven Story Pole.' It tells a story about a Native American tribal chief, his daughter, the sun, the moon, and the stars. This pole is the 'Bear Pole.' This pole tells the story about a bear that saved a man."

"**Harry,** our visit to Capilano Suspension Bridge Park was a lot of fun. I am glad we are back in our hotel so we can rest for a little while. We can enjoy the great view of the harbor, the mountains, the city, and Stanley Park from our hotel window."

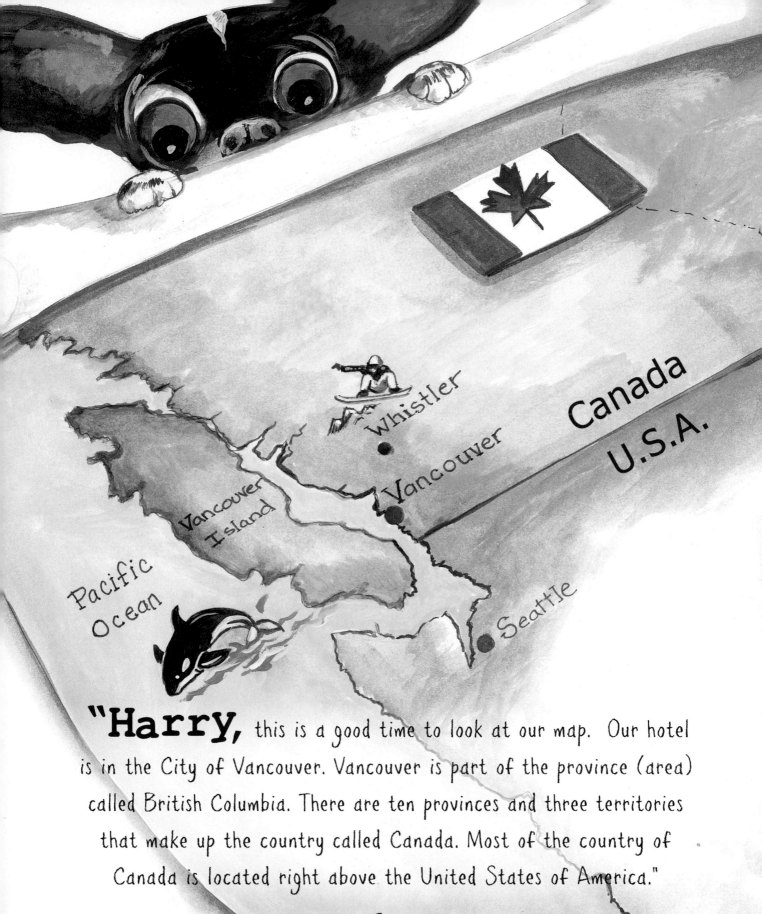

"**Harry,** this is a good time to look at our map. Our hotel is in the City of Vancouver. Vancouver is part of the province (area) called British Columbia. There are ten provinces and three territories that make up the country called Canada. Most of the country of Canada is located right above the United States of America."

19

"**Come** on, Harry. Let's head down to 'Gastown' for a snack. Gastown is the oldest part of the City of Vancouver."

"Look, Harry, that's a statue of John, 'Gassy Jack,' Deighton. He is considered the 'founding father' (or first resident) of Gastown, which is now part of Vancouver."

"Gassy...that's very funny, Bella! I don't smell anything."

"Oh, Harry, not that kind of gassy. He was called gassy because he was very, very talkative."

20

**"Bella,** look.

What is happening to the clock?"

"It's a steam clock, Harry."

22

"**Bella,** does that mean it is powered by steam?"

"Well, not exactly. This clock is powered by weights and is connected to a mini steam engine below ground, which has a motor. Every fifteen minutes, the clock whistles and shoots steam into the air. There are only a handful of steam clocks in the entire world."

**"Snack** time!"

"Bella, I really, really, really want to try some Canadian maple syrup."

"Okay, Harry, let's have some pancakes with Canadian maple syrup.
All of our *FUN* this morning has made me VERY hungry."

"Mmm...this is really good, Bella."

"**Harry,** did you know that Canadian maple syrup is made from the sap of a maple tree? Sap from sugar, red, black, and other types of maple trees can be used to make maple syrup."

"Nope, I just know it tastes really good."

25

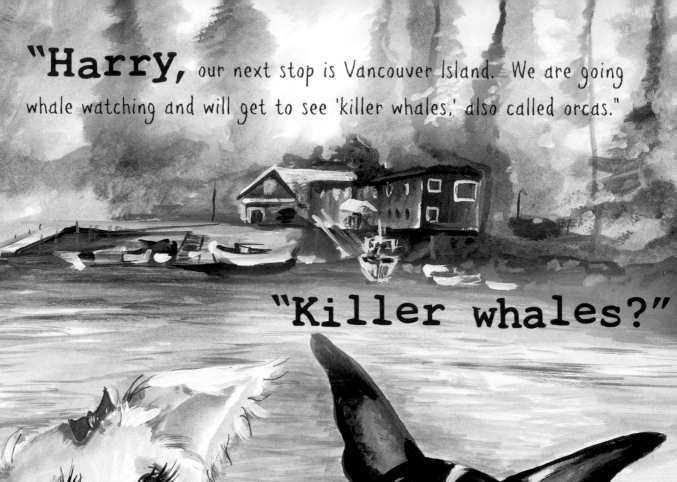

**"Harry,** our next stop is Vancouver Island. We are going whale watching and will get to see 'killer whales,' also called orcas."

"Killer whales?"

Vancouver Island

ORCA TOURS

"**Yes,** Harry. Each year, the whales swim near Vancouver Island while heading to a warmer place. The best time of year to see whales is from the beginning of April through October. Killer whales are the largest members of the dolphin family. The whales can grow as big as thirty feet long and weigh as much as 20,000 pounds."

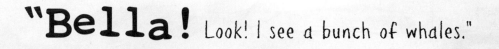

# "Bella! Look! I see a bunch of whales."

"Yes, Harry, that is called a 'pod' or a group. Most of the time whales swim as part of a pod. The whales swim very fast, too."

"**Look!** Look!"

"Bella, this is so much fun."

30

We had a great time whale watching, but now it is time to head back to the City of Vancouver. We hope you join us on our next adventure. For now, it's good-bye from Bella Boo and Harry too!

# Our Adventure to Vancouver

Bella and Harry visiting the Chinatown area of Vancouver.

Bella and Harry playing in Stanley Park.

Bella visiting the Whistler Blackcomb ski resort (about a two-hour drive from Vancouver) and skiing down Whistler Mountain.

Harry standing by the English Bay Inukshuk, located by the Vancouver Seawall.

# Common Canadian Words

Pop – Soda

Mounties – Policemen

Washroom – Restroom

Runners – Sneakers

Loonie – Canadian one-dollar coin

Toonie – Canadian two-dollar coin

Requests for permission to make copies of any part of the work should be directed to BellaAndHarryGo@aol.com or 855-235-5211.

Library of Congress Cataloging-in-Publications Data is available
Manzione, Lisa
The Adventures of Bella & Harry: Let's Visit Vancouver!

ISBN: 978-1-937616-54-0
First Edition
Book Fourteen of Bella & Harry Series

For further information please visit:
BellaAndHarry.com
or
Email: BellaAndHarryGo@aol.com

Printed in the United States of America
Phoenix Color, Hagerstown, Maryland
July 2014
14 7 14 PC 1 1